The Magic Weaver of Rugs

A Tale of the Navajo

Jerrie Oughton   Illustrated by Lisa Desimini

Houghton Mifflin Company
Boston 1994

This book is dedicated to
George Ella and Martha
Each a magic weaver of words
in her own unique way.
—J.O.

For My Sister Natalie
—L.D.

Text copyright © 1994 by Jerrie Oughton
Illustrations copyright © 1994 by Lisa Desimini

Library of Congress Cataloging-in-Publication Data

Oughton, Jerrie.
   The magic weaver of rugs / Jerrie Oughton ; illustrated by Lisa
Desimini.
      p.   cm.
   Summary: When two Navajo women pray for help for their cold and
hungry people, Spider Woman teaches them how to weave.
   ISBN 0-395-66140-4
   1. Navajo Indians—Legends.   [1. Navajo Indians—Legends.
2. Indians of North America—Legends.   3. Weaving—Folklore.]
I. Desimini, Lisa, ill.   II. Title.
E99.N3089   1994   93-4850
398.2'089972—dc20   CIP
[E]   AC

Printed in the United States of America

HOR   10   9   8   7   6   5   4   3   2   1

For the longest time, in the beginning, the people suffered from hunger and cold.

Even when winter had come and gone, it stayed winter in their hearts because the white wolf of fear crept among them. Fear that they would not survive. That they would die for lack of food and warmth.

At last, two women who could no longer stand by and watch their families suffer, traveled far from their camp to be alone and pray for help.

They traveled until they found themselves deep in a canyon. But they were not alone. High atop the canyon wall, Spider Woman looked down on them. The sandpaper wind stung her old skin as she walked along the edges of her homeland.

Spider Woman heard their prayers and had pity on them. Gathering all of her strength, she spun an iron-strong web and lassoed the two women, lifting them swiftly to her land near the sky.

"I have heard your pleas," she whispered in a voice that, full force, would have shattered rock.

"Who are you?" they asked.

"I am Spider Woman," she answered. "I have heard your pleas and brought you to me. Now you must do as I say and your needs will be met."

Saying this, she flung a spindle of steely web down to
a pine tree and uprooted it.

With one quick movement of her hand, she peeled off
the branches, leaving a slender pole.

She stabbed the pole into the ground atop the canyon.
Then she did the same with a second tree.

"I have built *up*," she whispered. "Next, I will build *across*."

When she had made a giant frame of the poles,
she spun her slender threads north and south.

"This is a loom," she told the two women.

"A loom?" they cried. "How can a loom keep us
warm in winter?"

"Take care you do not try my patience," Spider Woman whispered. Then, with a lightning flash of her hand, she lassoed the few sheep standing far below in the canyon. She sheared off their shaggy wool with her silver blade of a web.

Spider Woman showed the women how to wash and card the wool.

"But sheep wool cannot feed our people," they complained.

"Do you want my help?" Spider Woman called out in a voice that unleashed rocks from their nesting places.

The women cowered in fear. "Yes," they whispered.

"Then watch and do as I tell you," Spider Woman told them. "We will weave a rug."

They spun the wool into yarn.

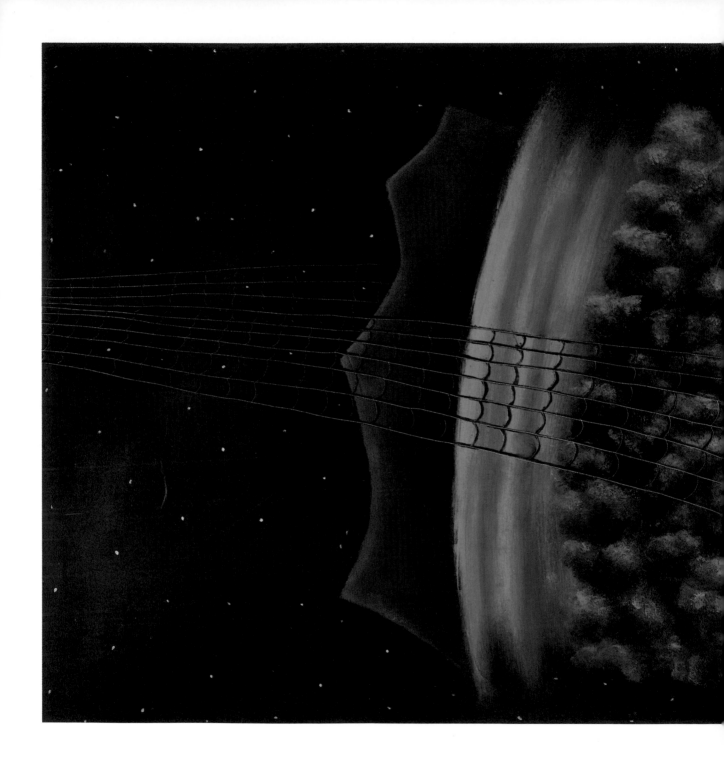

Then, with her silver web, Spider Woman
pulled colors from all the world.
Purple from the distant mountaintops.
Blue from the turquoise sky.
Green from pine branchlets.

Black from angry storm clouds.
Red from the sun-blistered desert sand.
White from the cold moon.
Yellow from the throat of a yucca plant.

The women dyed the wool as fast as Spider Woman gave
them the colors.

"Now," Spider Woman told them, "the moment has come
to weave." The women shuddered in fear, wondering what their
part would be in the weaving of a rug.

"It is IMPORTANT," Spider Woman thundered, bringing rain from the clouds. "Important to hold only beautiful thoughts in your mind while you weave a rug. Weave with your very souls and be sure to bind each end of the rug carefully."

And so they began to weave. Lacing the spun wool from east to west, then back again, weaving it in and out of the tall threads.

They wove day after day, passing the weft over and under the warps, using all the colors Spider Woman had drawn from their world. All the while, they held only beautiful thoughts in their heads.

But the days were long and the weaving tedious. Since Spider Woman had left them to their work, the women's thoughts wandered to their families. They could no longer hold beautiful thoughts when their minds had pictures of hungry children and family members suffering from the cold.

"She does not intend to help us," one of the women whispered to the other. "If she had left us in prayer, we might have gotten true help. Let us make a mistake in the weaving for revenge."

"Yes," the second woman agreed, "and let us also leave a small opening so that our souls will be able to escape."

When the rug was finished, Spider Woman came again, and the women said, "We have done as you asked. Now, will you help our people?"

"You are free to go," Spider Woman told them and set them once again on the canyon floor.

"But where is the help you promised?" they called up to her. "We thought only beautiful thoughts for many moons. We did as you asked. We wove your rug for you."

"The rug you wove is imperfect," Spider Woman called down to them, splitting the earth with her voice. "As well it should be, for you are mere mortals. Perfection is for the gods."

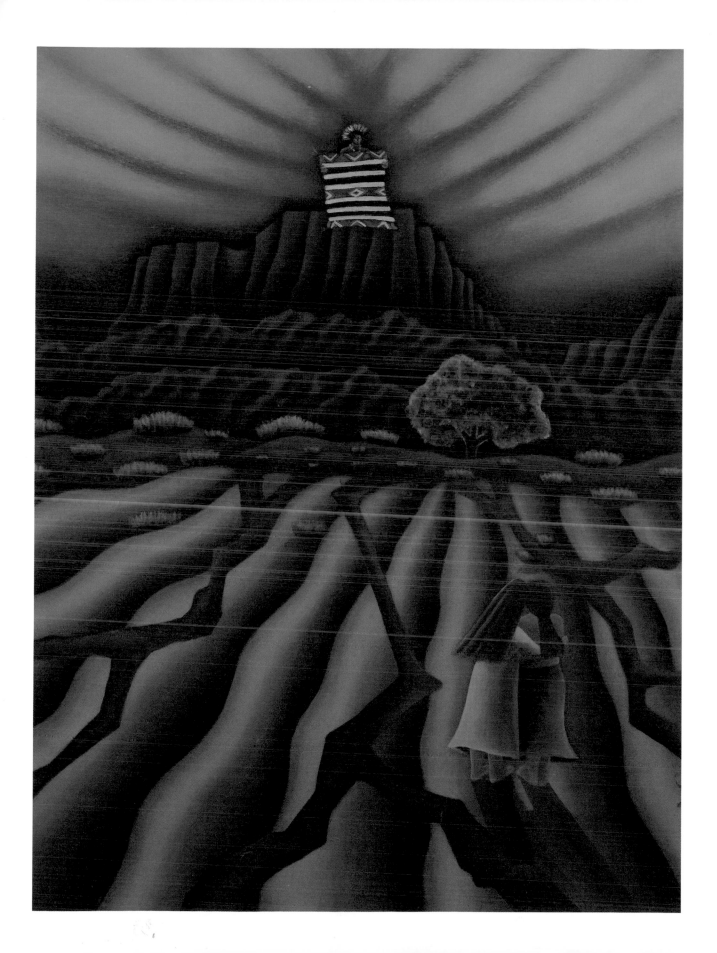

"At least give us the rug we wove," they cried.

"Your souls are not in this rug. You kept your souls. I will keep the rug," she roared.

The women fell to the ground in fear. Spider Woman looked at them trembling there and had mercy on them.

"The help you asked for will come," she told them. "The gift is already yours."

They began to weep. "But our people need help now," they cried. "Perhaps we need to go to a land that is kinder, where we can find food and warmth."

"You are of *this* place." Spider Woman's voice echoed back and forth in the canyon walls. "Let your minds make the journey!" And she was gone.

In despair, the women turned toward their family camp.
Their hearts were heavy because they thought they were
returning with no more help than they had when they had

begun their journey. To ease their suffering, they began
teaching the people to gather wool and color it with dyes
and weave the wool into rugs.

The people wove and wove. They wove for themselves
and for their families. They drew even more colors from the
land and wove patterns out of their heads.

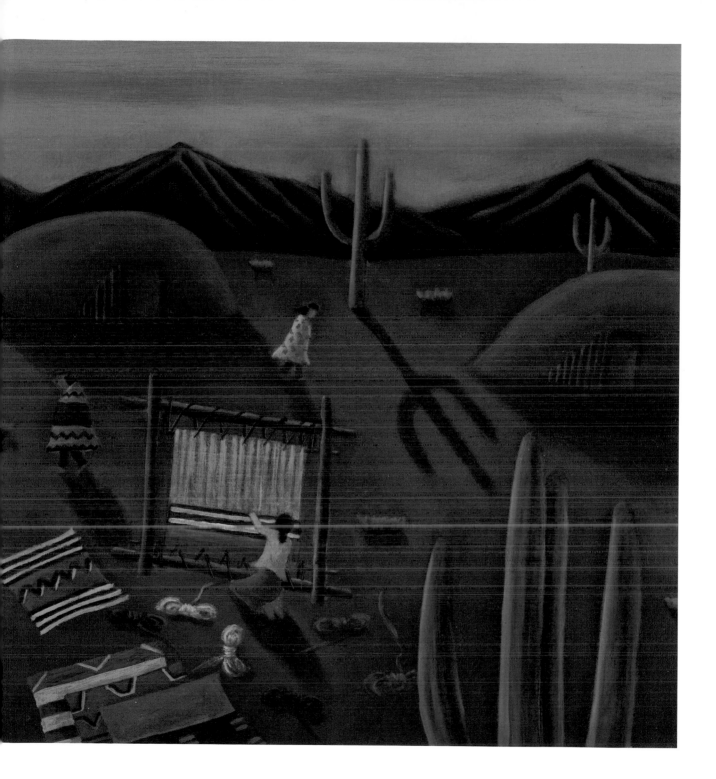

They traded the rugs for food and warm animal skins,
and prosperity began to fill their lives.

Many moons later the two women returned to thank
Spider Woman. Finding the lonely canyon that rested at
the foot of her homeland, they called and called to her.
But she did not come.